Journey to Magic Island

By Michael Teitelbaum
Illustrated by Darrell Baker

A GOLDEN BOOK • NEW YORK

Western Publishing Company, Inc., Racine, Wisconsin 53404

©1989 The Walt Disney Company. All rights reserved. Printed in the U.S.A. No part of this book may be reproduced or copied in any form without written permission from the copyright owner. GOLDEN, GOLDEN & DESIGN, A GOLDEN BOOK, A GOLDEN LOOK-LOOK BOOK, and A GOLDEN LITTLE LOOK-LOOK BOOK are trademarks of Western Publishing Company, Inc. Library of Congress Catalog Card Number: 88-51402 ISBN: 0-307-11754-5/ISBN: 0-307-61774-2 (lib. bdg.)   MCMXCI

One afternoon Huey, Dewey, and Louie were playing baseball outside McDuck Mansion. Right in the middle of the game Uncle Scrooge came rushing over. He was very excited.

"Look at this, boys," shouted Scrooge. "I think this time I'm onto something big! I just read about an amazing place in my *International Geographic* magazine."

Scrooge showed the boys the article. "It's a place called Magic Island," said Scrooge. "Everything on the island has magical powers. Just think—I could make a fortune if I went there and brought back magic objects to sell!"

"But, Uncle Scrooge," said Huey, "you
already *have* a fortune!"

"It never hurts to have a spare," said Scrooge
with a smile.

Scrooge and his nephews soon found their trusty pilot, Launchpad McQuack. "Get the helicopter ready to fly, Launchpad," said Scrooge. "We're off in search of magic!"

"Right away, Mr. McD.," responded Launchpad.

After a long flight in Launchpad's helicopter, the ducks finally spotted Magic Island. "There it is!" shouted Scrooge.

Launchpad brought the helicopter down for one of his typical landings.

"Everyone okay?" asked Scrooge. They all said that they were fine. "Then let's get going!" Scrooge said.

The ducks gathered up their gear and began to explore the island.

The explorers arrived at the entrance to a cave. A strange, magical glow was coming from inside it.

"Magic!" exclaimed Huey.

"Wow!" said Dewey.

"Come on," added Louie. "Let's go in."

Once inside the cave, they discovered the source of the glow. "Magic stones!" said Scrooge with delight. "And they're all mine!"

"Oh, no, they're not, Scrooge!" exclaimed a voice from behind them. "They're *mine!*"

"Magica De Spell!" the nephews shouted together. "What are you doing here?"

"The same thing as you," said the evil sorceress. "This is *my* island, Scrooge. I got here first. I'll see to it that you are nothing more than a very *small* interruption in my work.

"The magic on this island has increased my powers," continued Magica. "Watch."

Magica held one of the stones over her head. A magic glow from the stone surrounded the ducks.

"Hey, I feel strange," said Launchpad.

"Look, Uncle Scrooge," said Dewey. "We're all getting smaller!"

Magica's spell had shrunk the explorers down to a tiny size.

The tiny ducks turned and ran out of the cave,
away from the giant Magica. Once they were
outside, a chilly breeze made them shiver.

"I'm freezing, Mr. McD.," Launchpad said.

Huey spotted a fallen leaf from a nearby tree.
"Maybe this will help keep us warm," he said.
The ducks wrapped the leaf around them.

"I wish we were normal size again," moaned
Dewey.

POOF! No sooner had Dewey made his wish than the ducks returned to their normal size.

"That must have been a magical leaf," said Louie. "It made your wish come true!"

"Shh, be very, very quiet," said Scrooge as the group sneaked back into the cave. While Magica had her back to him, Scrooge picked up one of the magic stones.

"You're not the only one who can use the
magic on this island, Magica," said Scrooge as he
held the stone above his head. Scrooge wished
that Magica were off the island and back at her
home. Magic energy flew from the stone and
surrounded Magica. Before she could move, the
power of the stone made her vanish.

"You did it, Uncle Scrooge!" cheered the nephews.

"Now let's fill up this sack with magic stones and be on our way," said Scrooge.

Back at the mansion, Scrooge gathered
everyone around for a demonstration of how the
stones worked. He pulled a stone out of his bag
and held it up.

"I wish for a huge pile of gold coins," Scrooge said. Nothing happened. Then Scrooge noticed the stone wasn't glowing anymore.

"I can't believe it!" said Scrooge. "The magic is gone. I wonder why."

"Look at this, Uncle Scrooge," said Huey. "It says here, at the end of the magazine article, that the magic objects lose their power when they are taken away from Magic Island."

"I was in such a hurry to leave for the island, I never finished the article," Scrooge said with a sigh. "I guess I'll have to get along with only one fortune, after all."